"HERE KITTY, KITTY..." THE SEQUEL

Living the good life (theirs, not yours)

TEXT AND ILLUSTRATIONS BY

RICHARD DOMMERS

PINNACLE BOOKS

PINNACLE BOOKS are published by

Kensington Publishing Corp.
850 Third Avenue
New York, NY 10022

Copyright © 1995 by Richard W. Dommers, Jr.

All rights reserved. No part of this book may by reproduced in any form or by any means without the prior written consent of the Publisher, excepting brief quotes used in reviews.

If you purchased this book without a cover, you should be aware that this book is stolen property. It was reported as "unsold and destroyed" to the Publisher and neither the Author nor the Publisher has received any payment for this "stripped book."

Pinnacle and the P logo Reg. U.S. Pat. & TM Off.

First Printing: July, 1996
10 9 8 7 6 5 4 3 2 1

Printed in the United States of America

ACKNOWLEDGMENTS

Thank you to all of my family's cats while I was growing up: Dolly (Fibbles), Scally, Foos Foos, Wilma, Ginger (Boozer), Pixie, Spike, Groucho, Fatty, and all the rest of the gang. I have spent nearly my entire life observing these quite delightful and sometimes annoying creatures from kittenhood to the end of their ninth lives. The funny and annoying things they did, and some of the strange and humorous situations they got themselves into, are the basis for this book.

Thank you to my wife for her many contributions; to my family, for their support; to Peter Lombard, for his ideas and fine-tuned sense of humor; to Tony C., for helping me add more to some of the cartoons; to Lynn Ann, for an idea or two; to Ann LaFarge, Karen Haas, and Elise Donner, for all the help in bringing substance to this book; and to Joseph Ajlouny and Gwen Foss, who provided a pathway for the success of this and *Here Kitty, Kitty*.

Also, thank you, Kevin Geenty, for letting me use your office and equipment to produce my manuscripts.

To all of the disc jockeys and media people who supported *Here Kitty, Kitty* and appreciated it for what it is (just humor), thank you!

CONTENTS

Introduction		7
1:	Practical Jokes to Play on Your Cat	9
2:	I Could Kill My Cat!	37
3:	Funny Things Cats Do	81
4:	Having Fun with Your Cat	101
5:	Kitties and Kiddies	109
6:	Cute as a Kitten	127
7:	Kitty Fears	141

The pranks depicted in this book are an expression of cat humor, not cat care. Please be good to your feline friends, and perhaps they will meow a little less loudly.

INTRODUCTION

Well, here it is—the sequel to *"Here Kitty, Kitty..." Practical Jokes to Play on Your Cat!* However, this time it's a mixed bag of humor. For all of you who liked the last book, I didn't get too soft, and I have included more tasteless practical jokes and off-color cartoons. For all who hated my last book... well, you'll hate this one, too!

Too bad!

CHAPTER 1

Practical Jokes to Play on Your Cat

Dangle or Die

Carry your cat into a yard full of ferocious dogs. Place your cat in a tree so that it is hanging from a tree branch by his front paws at a height just out of reach of the dogs.

Kitty Rescue

Sometimes cats get stuck in trees. To "rescue" them, make a platform out of wood framing with a thin paper platform. Place it under the tree and encourage your cat to jump.

Fish Bowl Surprise

If your cat has the bad habit of eating your poor defenseless little goldfish, then try evening the odds. Replace the goldfish with piranhas.

Bad Takeoff

As your cat begins to leap from a chair, pull the chair away. Instead of reaching his destination, he will fall to the floor.

Missed Landing

As your cat is about to jump onto a chair, pull it away. Your cat will contort and even make faces as it tries to adjust for a less than perfect landing.

Cream Cheese Kitty

For some light entertainment, place a small dab of cream cheese on your cat's nose. Your cat will go cross-eyed while sticking its tongue out numerous times as it tries to devour the cream cheese.

Pole Cat

Lure a cat to a metal flagpole in subzero weather by putting a piece of tuna on it. The cat will do the rest.

Catnip Collar

Test your cat's bravery by making a collar from catnip and placing it around your dog's neck.

Cactus Kitty

If your cat is one which likes to chew on your plants, try adding a cactus to your collection. Coat it with fish oil.

All Juiced Up

Try splashing some beef broth on the sharp edge of a cleaver and leave the knife near your cat's favorite kitchen spot.

Sniffer Snap

Simply give your cat a static shock on its nose.
P.S. This only works once, so make it a big one!

Garage Gag

Tie your cat to the automatic garage door ... but make sure there are fresh batteries in the remote opener!

Toilet Paper Chase

Tie the end of a roll of toilet paper to your cats tail and let 'em rip!

CHAPTER 2

I Could Kill My Cat!

Critter Corpses

Cats love to show off their hunting ability by bringing their dead quarry home. If that isn't enough, they decapitate and gut the little critters and drop them on the porch.

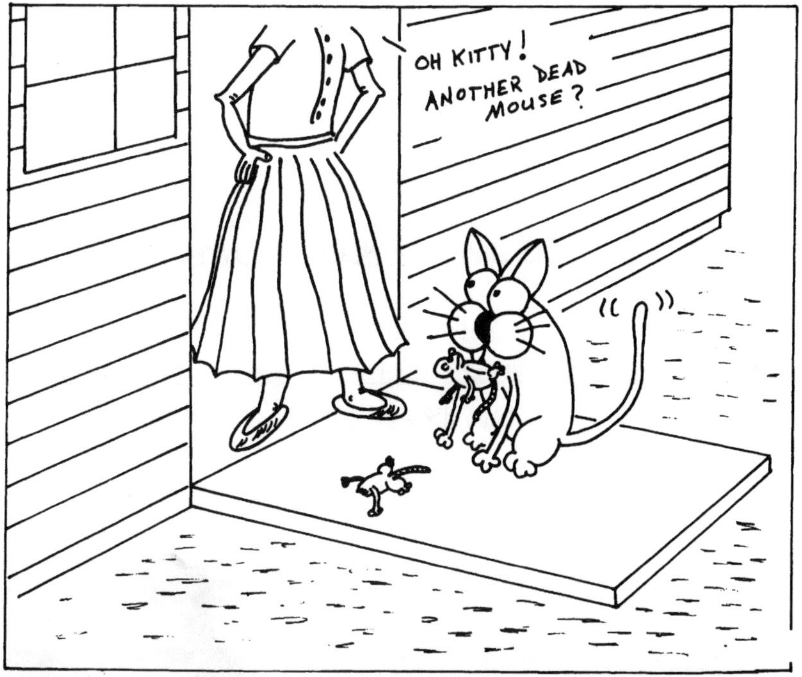
OH KITTY! ANOTHER DEAD MOUSE?

Home away from Home

Does your cat disappear for days, even weeks at a time? Cats do this because they have alternate lives with other families.

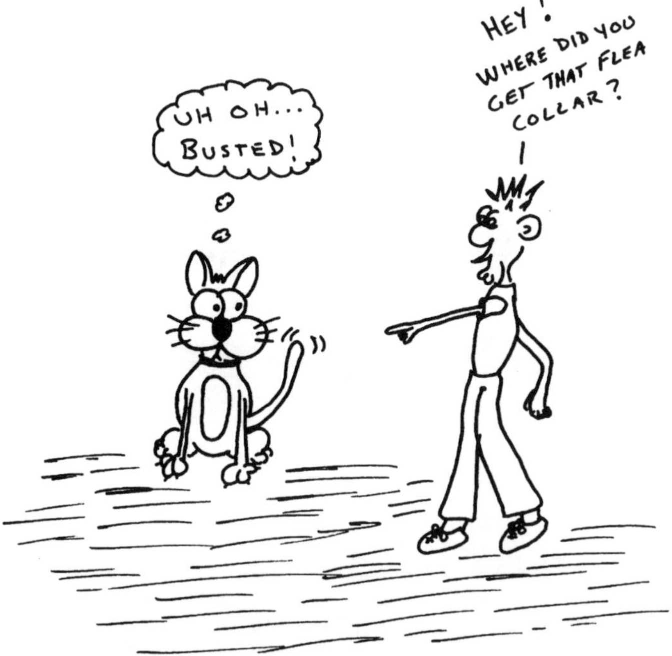
UH OH...
BUSTED!
HEY!
WHERE DID YOU GET THAT FLEA COLLAR?

Feline Face Mask

There's nothing like removing a cat from your face while you try to sleep!

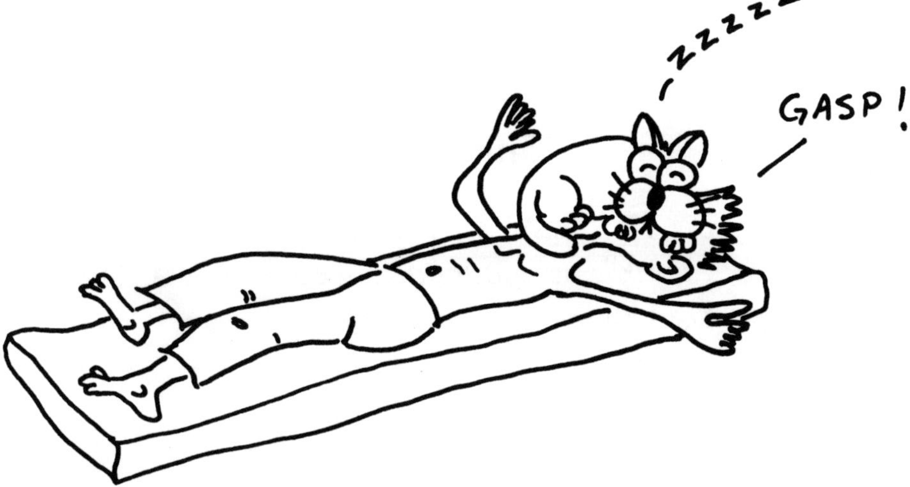
ZZZZZZ
GASP!

"Curtains"

Ohhh, yes ... that all-too-familiar sound of *"rip ... clunk"* as your cat tears down the drapes. Bad kitty!

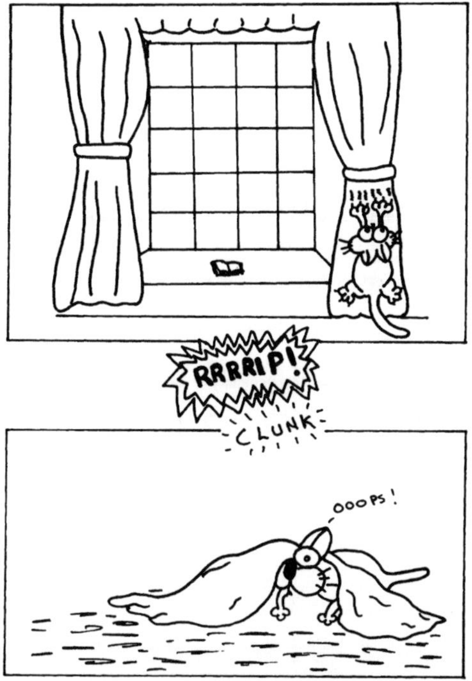
RRRRIP!
CLUNK
OOOPS!

Batting Practice

Cats like to play with string, and they keep in practice by batting the cords hanging from the window blinds. What your cat doesn't know is that those cords have a purpose other than batting practice.

47

Christmas Kitty

Cats think Christmas is just for them. No wonder cats destroy Christmas decorations!

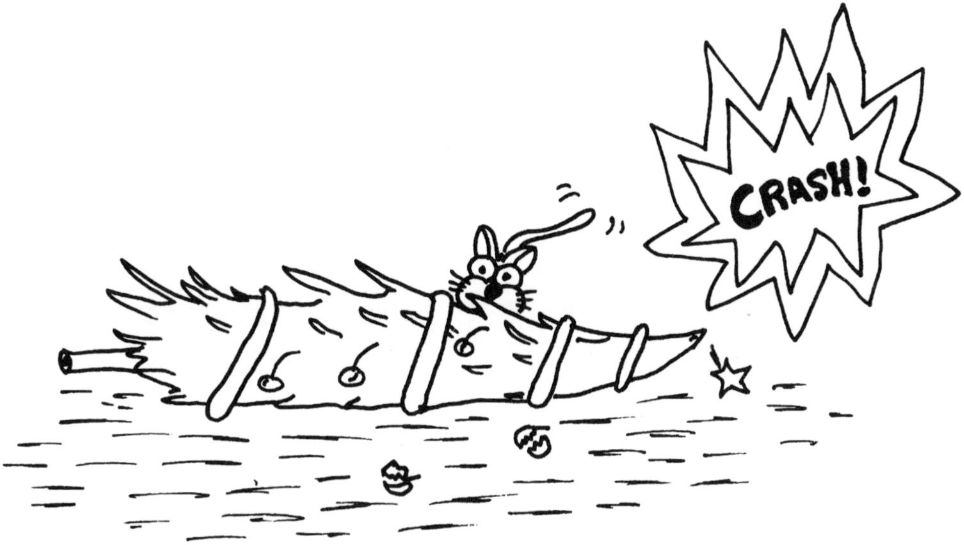
CRASH!

Yarn Ball

Cats just love to interrupt a perfectly good knitting project by messing up the yarn! It's something for them to play with and, at the same time, it could potentially annoy the knitter.

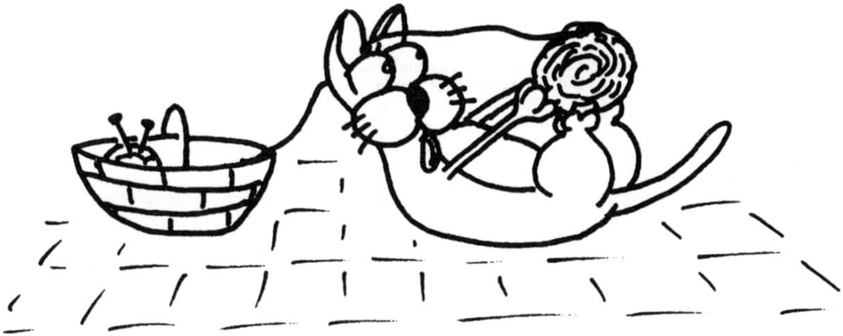

Alternate Scratching Post

The furniture ... cats shred it with their claws. The more expensive the furniture, the faster and harder they destroy it!

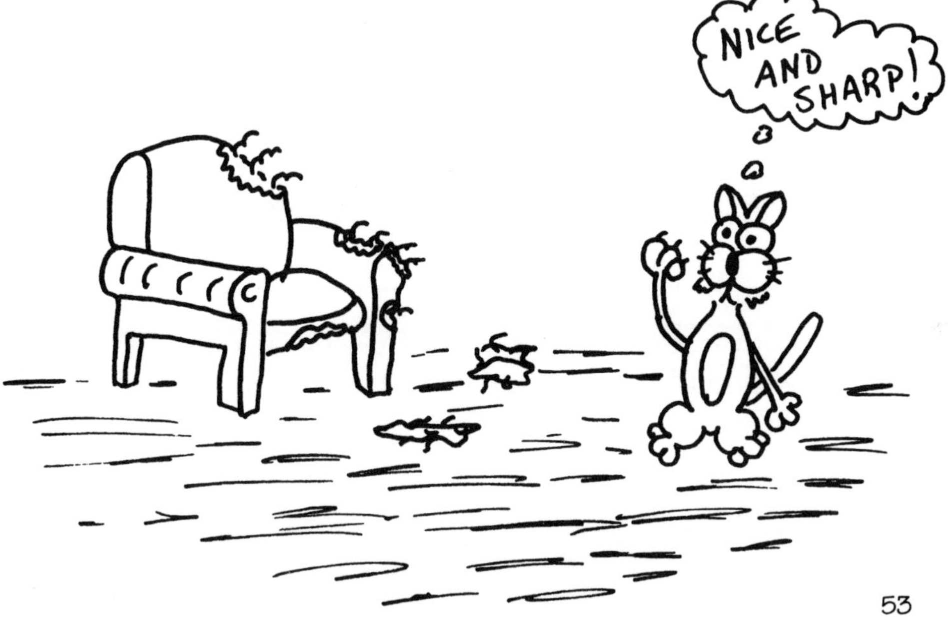
NICE AND SHARP!

Fertilizing the Plant

Why do cats avoid their litter boxes and use the planters? Do they feel closer to nature? Do they hate the plant? Or is it just more fun?

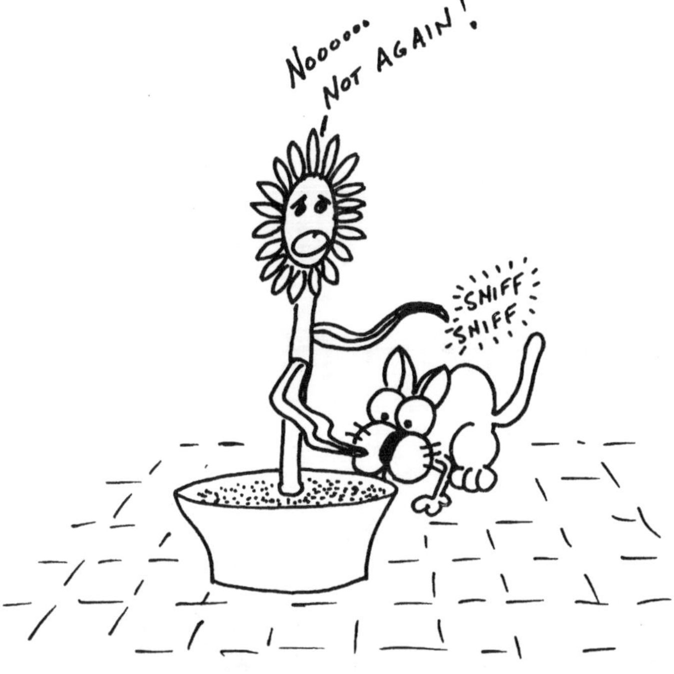
NOOOOOO NOT AGAIN!
SNIFF SNIFF

Plant Tipping

Plant Tipping is a favorite pastime for bored housecats.

Warm Nap

Ever wonder why there is so much kitty fur stuck to your clean laundry?

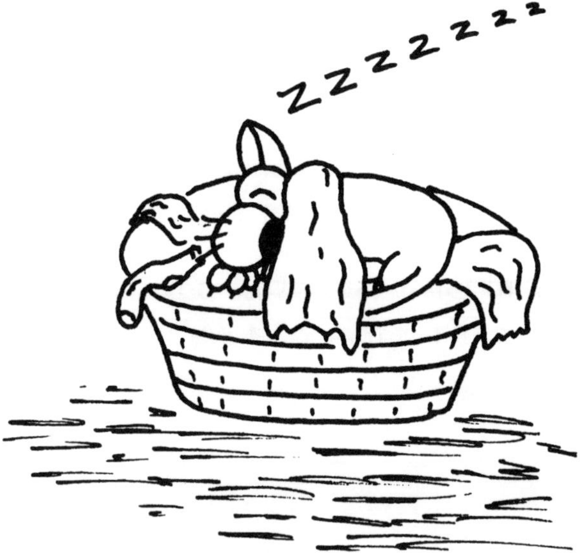
Z Z Z Z Z Z Z Z

Death-Defying Pawprints

Even the most frustrated car owner will not dare rile a cat for fear of a scratched paint job!

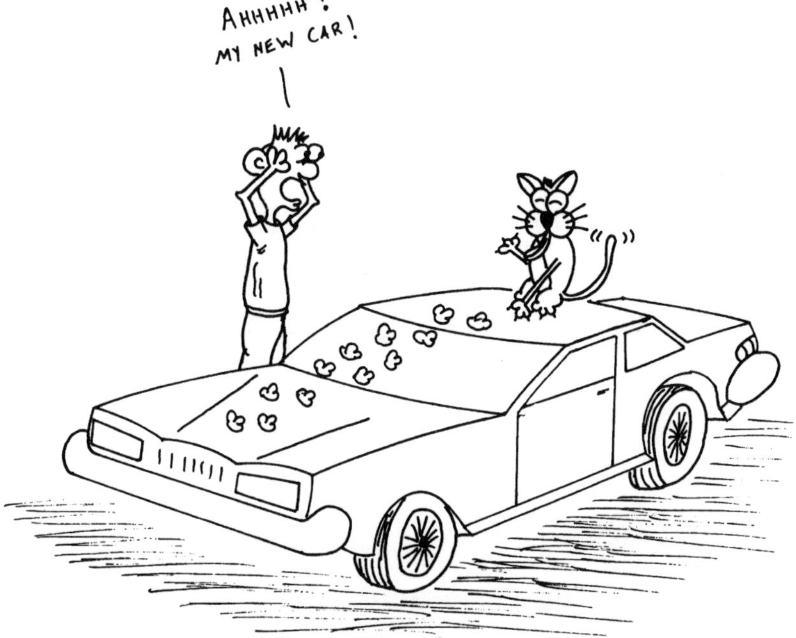
AHHHHH!
MY NEW CAR!

Alley Cat Wannabes

These are the suburban cats, who live good lives in warm homes with lots of food, yet they still raid the garbage.

63

Taking Down the Laundry

A torn brassiere and shredded stockings can only be the work of your cat. Cats will rise to meet the challenge of pulling down the articles of clothing you hang on your shower curtain rod, and in the process, ripping and shredding results. Boy ... doesn't that make you mad?

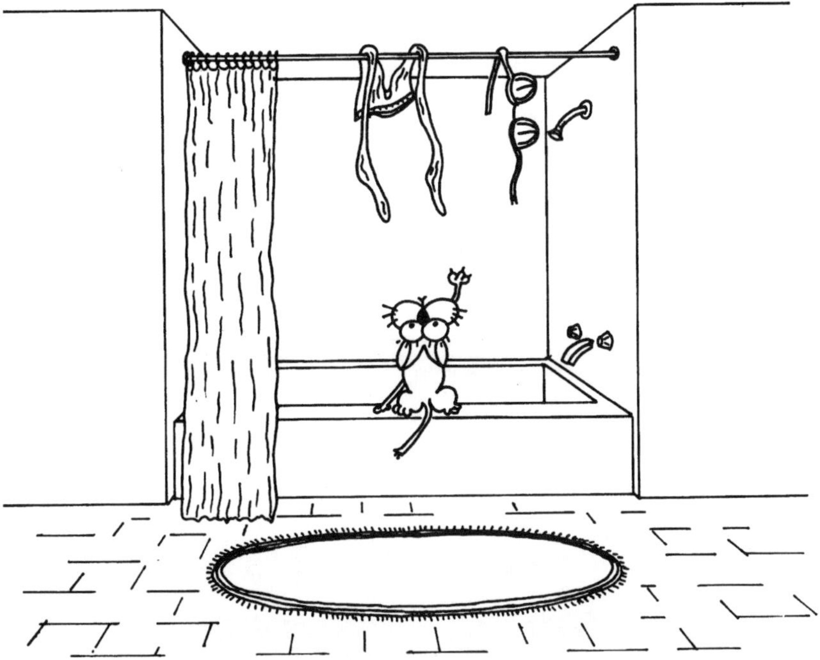

Counter Kitty

Most cats will jump onto the counter despite the severe punishments. Next time ... get him really good!

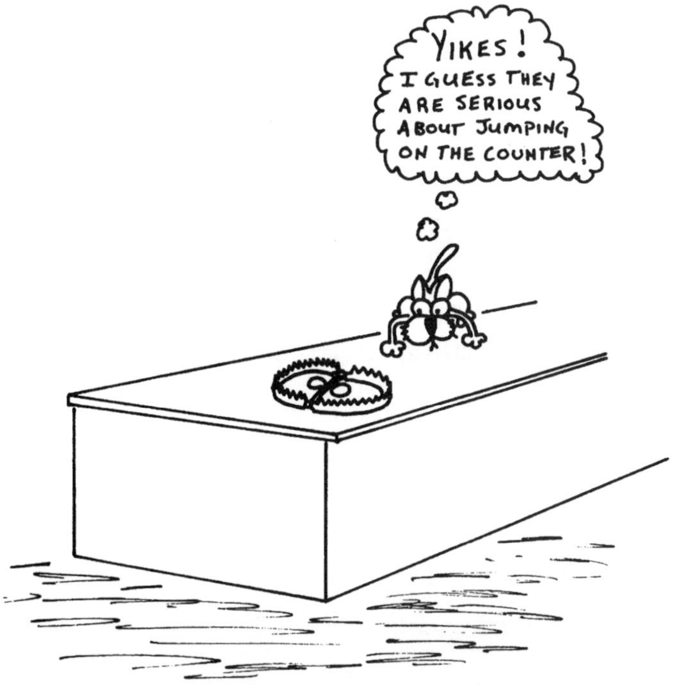
YIKES!
I GUESS THEY ARE SERIOUS ABOUT JUMPING ON THE COUNTER!

No Silverware?

Cats sneak behind your back and eat from the plates on the table and the pots and pans on the stove.

How gross!

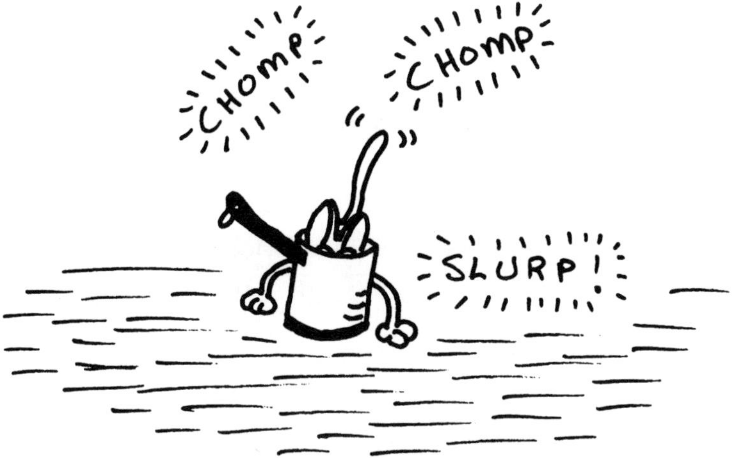
CHOMP
CHOMP
SLURP!

Oops!

Cats make the worst messes around their litter boxes. Cats sometimes balance on the edge, trying not to get their feet messy. And, they miss.

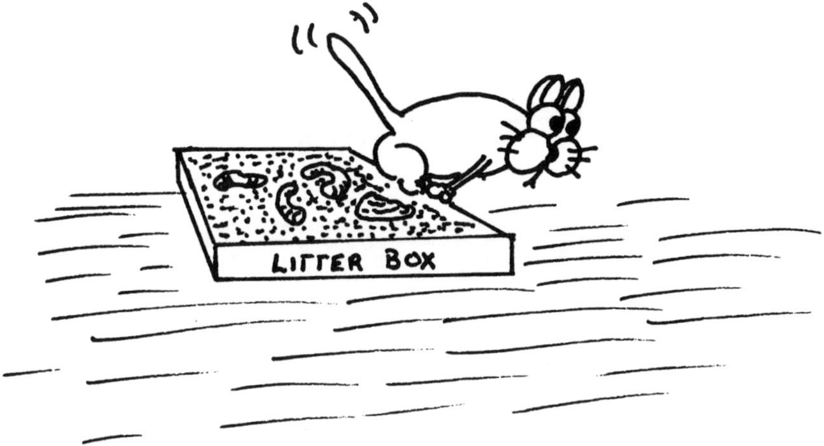
LITTER BOX

Hairball Hell

Those furry projectiles your cat leaves all over the house, sometimes on the very seats you sit in . . . yuck!

73

Fleas, Fleas, Fleas

Fleas, a thankless gift from your cat!

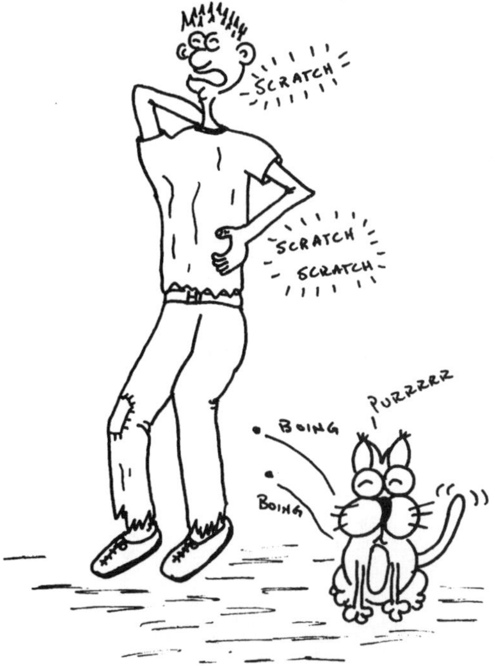
SCRATCH
SCRATCH
SCRATCH
PURRRRR
BOING
BOING

Bird Feeder Frenzy

What a fun pastime ... terrorizing the poor little birdies in the hopes of catching one for a meal. However, sometimes a free meal is worth the risk, even when the birds fight back!

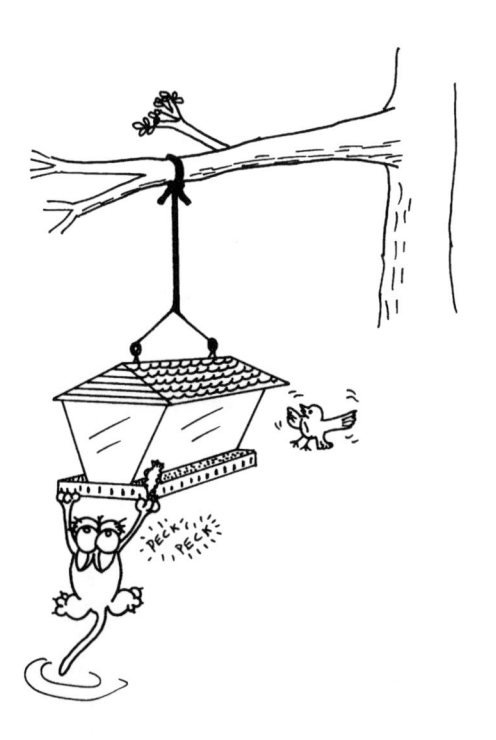

Littering

This is when your cat pops out a litter of kittens in the back of your closet, so far back that it takes weeks just to find them.

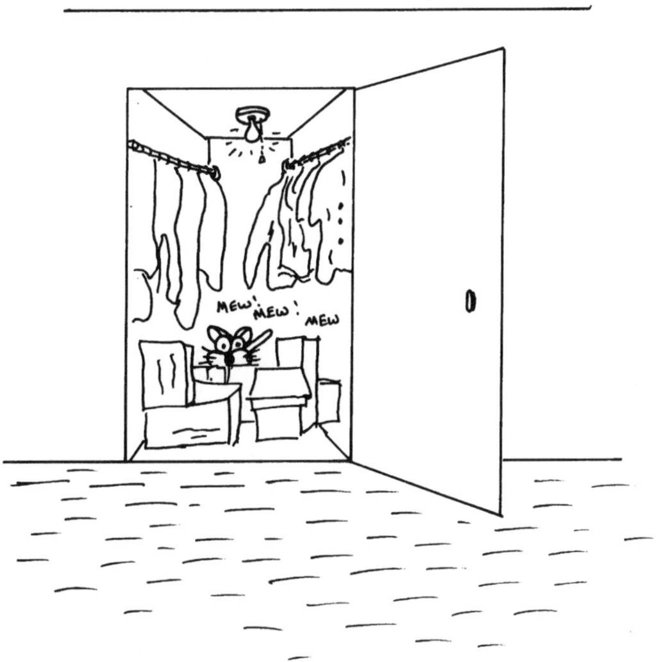
MEW!
MEW!
MEW

CHAPTER 3

Funny Things Cats Do

Cobweb Kitty

Sometimes crawling through tight spots in the attic will produce a messy coating of cobwebs. These don't lick off too easily.

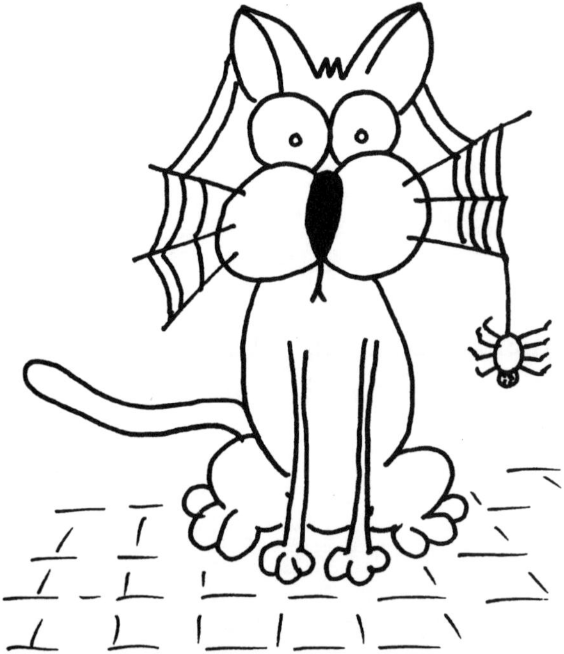

Wash Me

Sometimes cats will lick their owners to include them in the cat's bathing ritual.

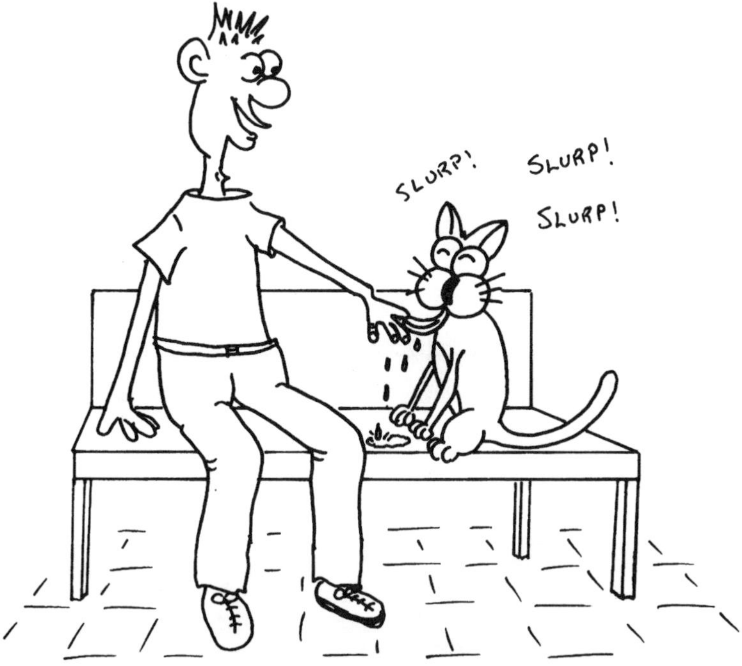
SLURP!
SLURP!
SLURP!

Fat Cats

Ever wonder what cats dream about? Milk, cheese, meat, catnip, cream, ice cream, and stuff like that. If you gave your cats all these treats, they would eat until they popped.

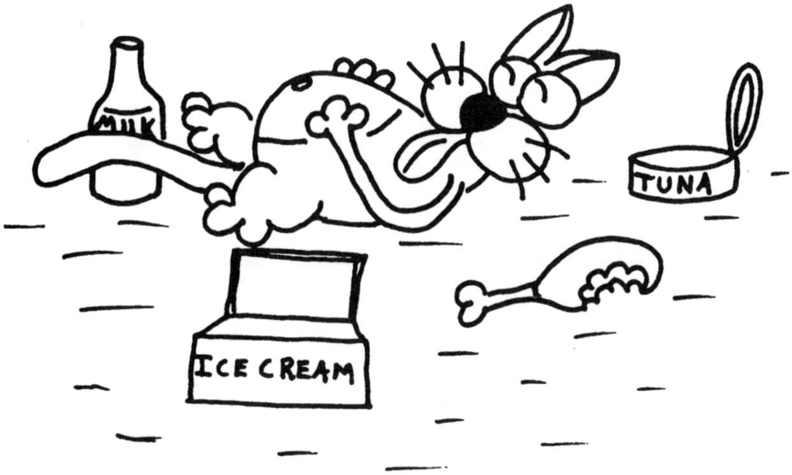
MILK
TUNA
ICE CREAM

Catnip Delight

Catnip makes cats dopey. It's a treat to see them lose control.

WOAH
LITTLE KITTEN DUDE...
TRY THIS GROOVY
NIP!
CAT NIP
SNIFF
SNIFF

Spot in the Sun

Some cats' only exercise is to migrate with the sun spot.

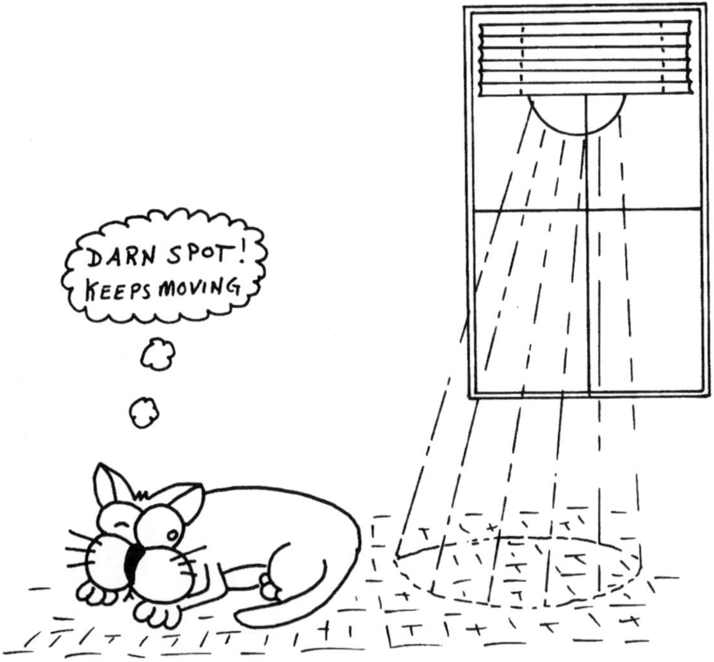
DARN SPOT! KEEPS MOVING

Monday Night Football

Some cats take an interest in sporting activities, and batting at the football players on the television is one of them!

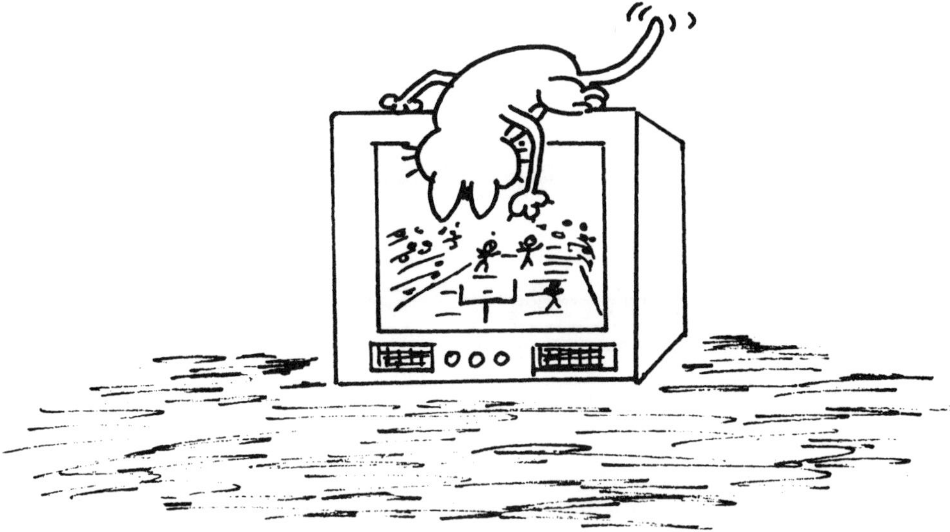

Riling Rover

It doesn't take more than a few sharp claws to earn the dog's respect. Hey, isn't the cat supposed to fear the dog?

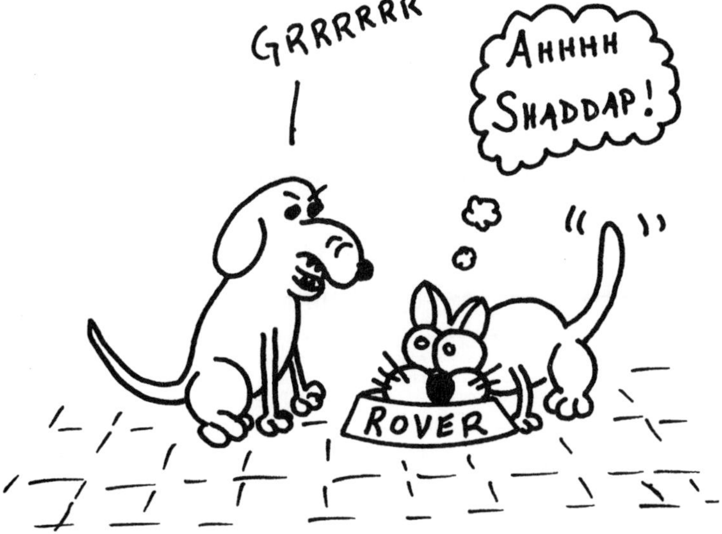
GRRRRRRR
AHHHH SHADDAP!
ROVER

Loose Laces

In an effort to entertain themselves, cats will play with shoelaces. Sometimes they even untie them.

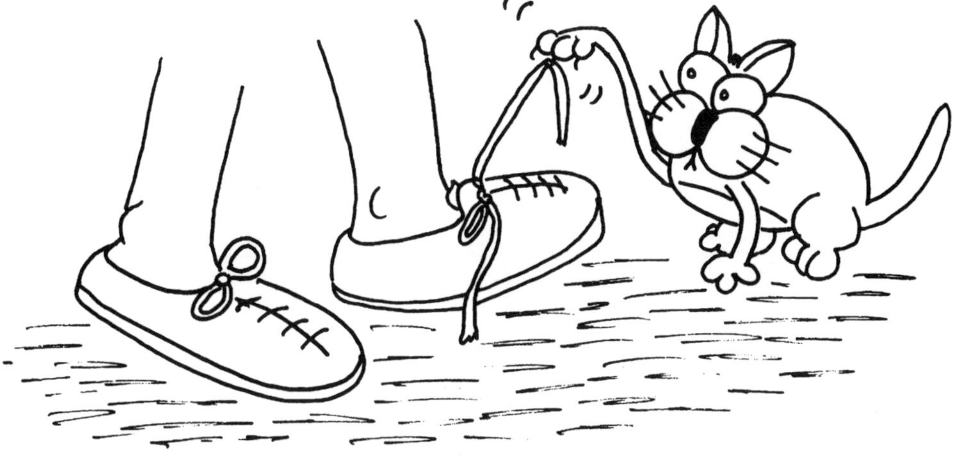

Here, Catch!

Unlike dogs, most cats will not catch things in their mouths when tossed to them.

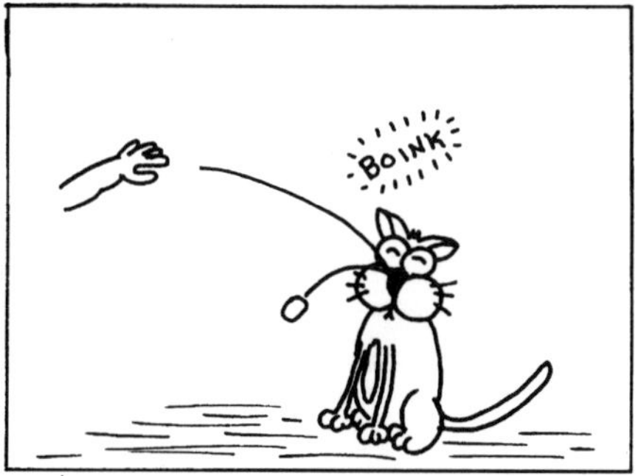
BOINK

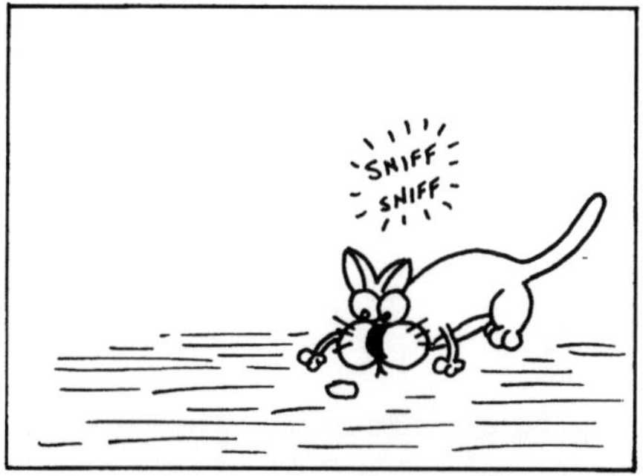
SNIFF
SNIFF

CHAPTER 4

Having Fun with Your Cat

Kitty TV

Cut a face hole out of a small- to medium-sized paper bag, so that when placed over a sitting cat, the cat can look out. When your cat takes a seat, place the bag over your cat. Most cats will sit in place indefinitely until the bag is removed, while others will try to escape. For full effect, draw knobs and speakers onto the bag to make it look like a TV.

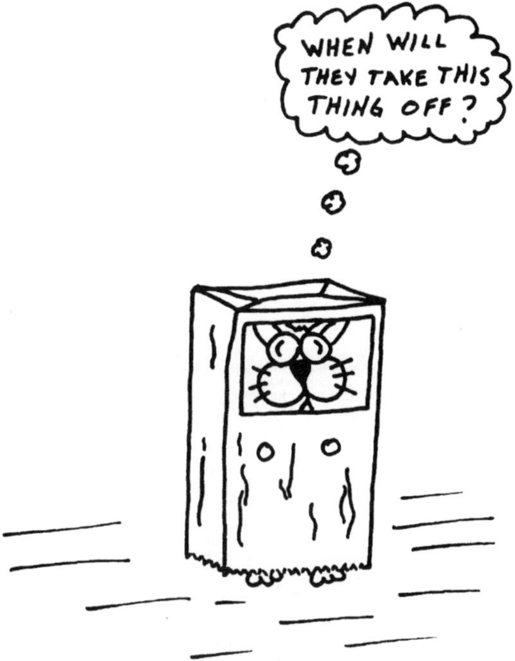
WHEN WILL THEY TAKE THIS THING OFF?

Rug Rider

When your cat steps onto an area rug, grab an end of the rug and swing it around in circles over a slippery floor. Your cat will either bail off or hang on for its life.

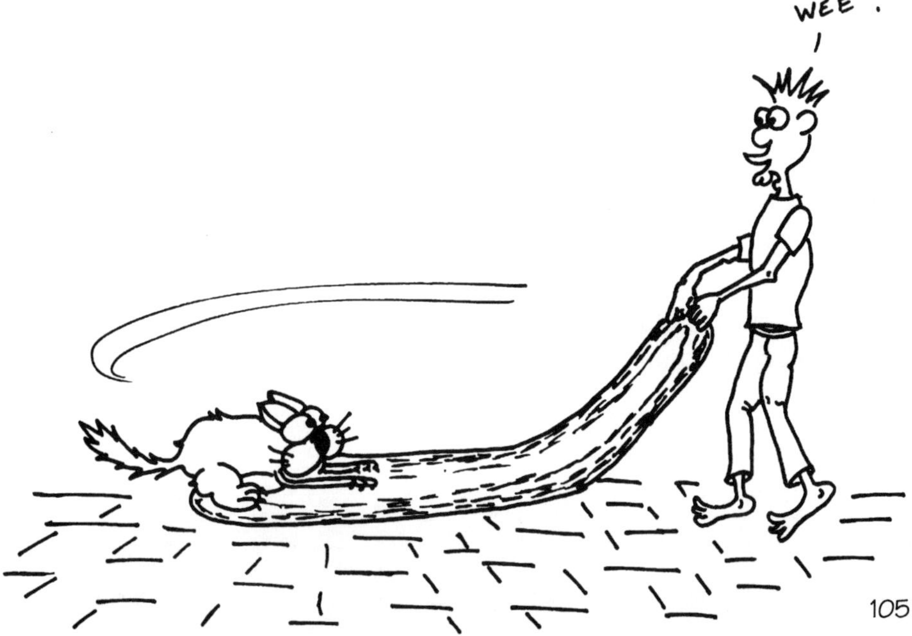
WEE!

Peeping Tomcat

The next time your cat peeps at you in the bathtub, give him a good splash!

SPLASH!

107

CHAPTER 5

Kitties and Kiddies

I Love My Kitty!

Let's face it, toddlers typically love their cats. The cats, however, have a hard time absorbing this much love at once.

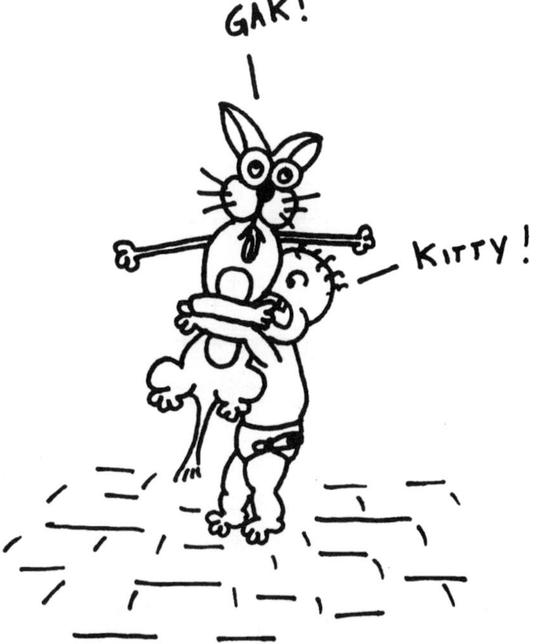
GAK!
KITTY!

Tail Torture

A cat will pull away if its tail has been grabbed. When toddlers grab a cat's tail, not only does the cat pull, but so does the toddler. OUCH!

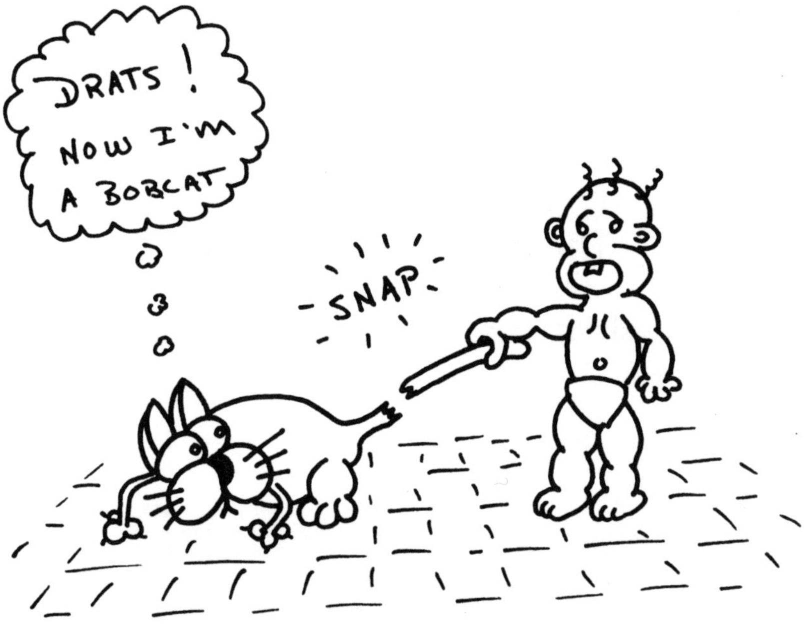
DRATS! NOW I'M A BOBCAT
SNAP

The Whisker Stretch

To kids, whiskers are just another bit of kitty equipment to yank on.

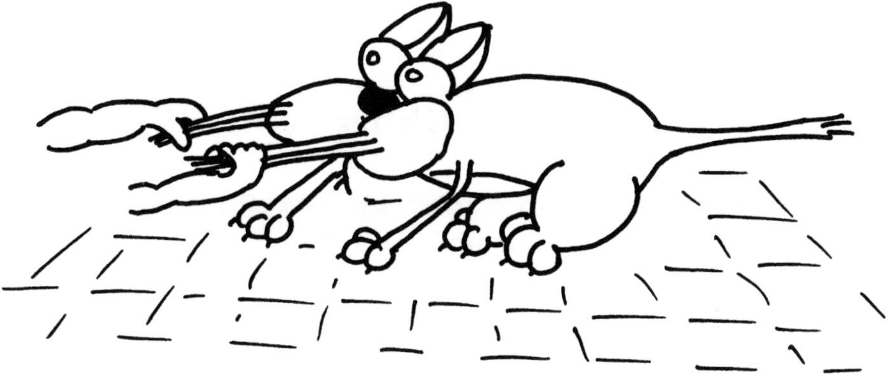

Close Shave

What happens when a toddler gets a brand new set of safety scissors? Poor kitty.

The Chase

A playful toddler and a new tyke bike are a dangerous combination for the family cat.

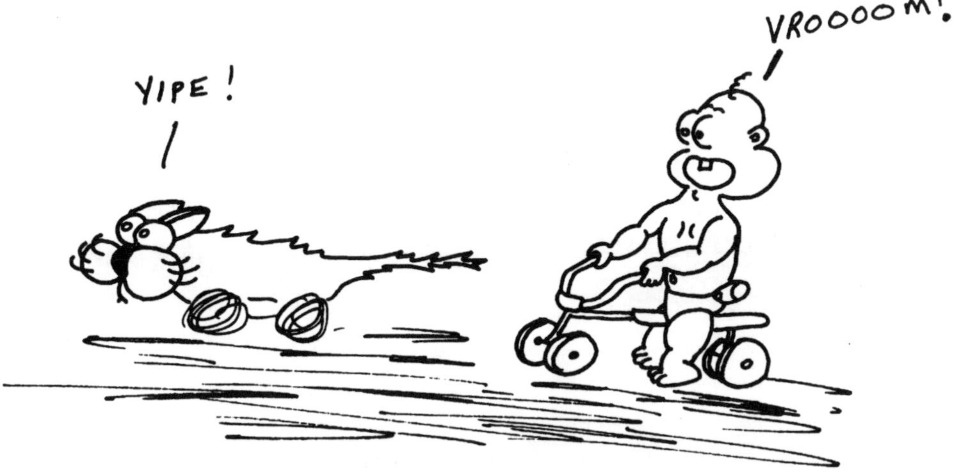
YIPE!
VROOOOM!

Hunting Tigers

Rubber knives can bring a wealth of adventure to a toddler. With a stretch of the imagination, the cat becomes a fierce, hunted tiger!

121

Bombs Away

Cats make good targets for gooey, half-eaten cookies.

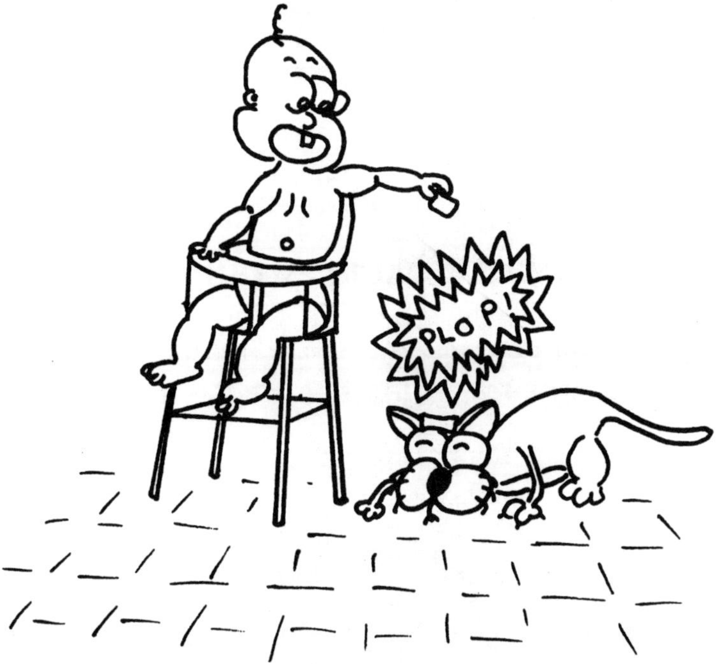
PLOP!

Just Poking Around

Toddlers will poke at many of the cat's orifices, mostly when the cat least expects it.

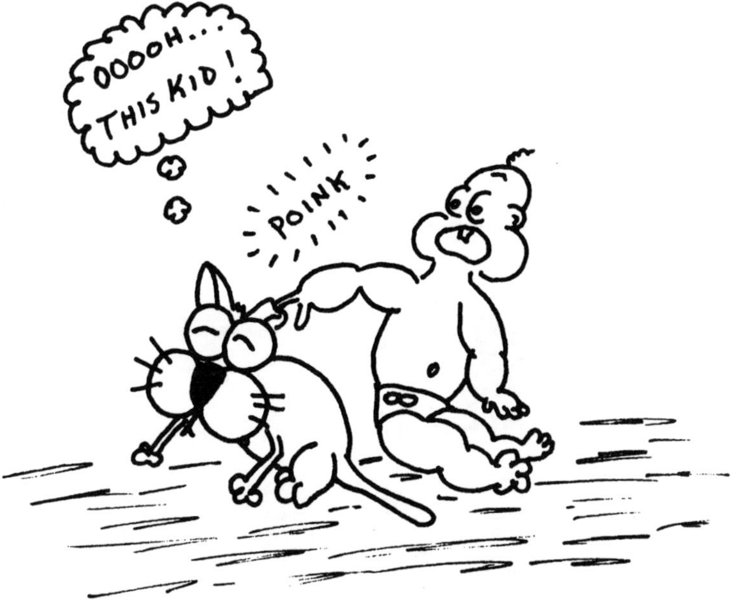
OOOOH...
THIS KID!
POINK

Coochy-Coo!

When the cat's asleep is the best time for your toddler to tickle its nose with its tail.

CHAPTER 6

Cute as a Kitten

Wobble Wobble

Kittens wobble a lot when they first start walking—an amusing sight to see as they make their way to unexplored territory ... especially on a shiny, waxed floor.

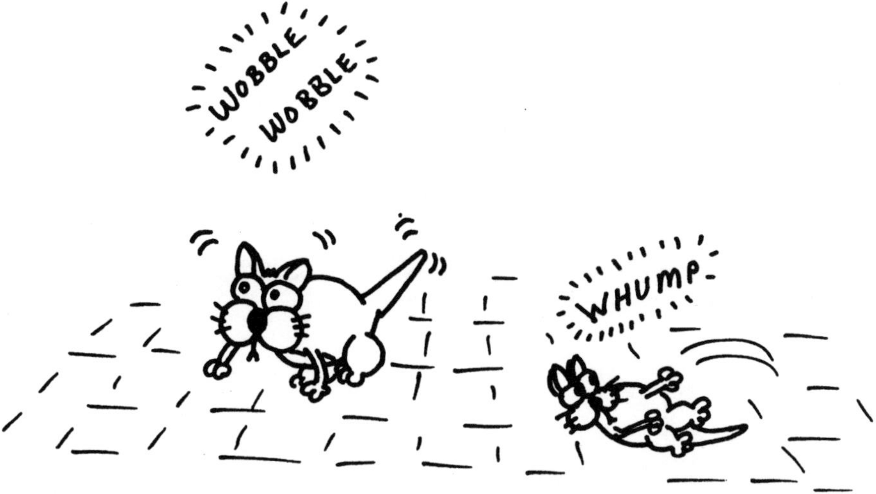
WOBBLE
WOBBLE
WHUMP

Mew?

What are those kittens really trying to say as they open their little mouths?

King of the Mountain

One of the first adventures kittens have is climbing to the top of Mom Cat. It is not unusual to see them knock each other off and roll down all five inches to the floor.

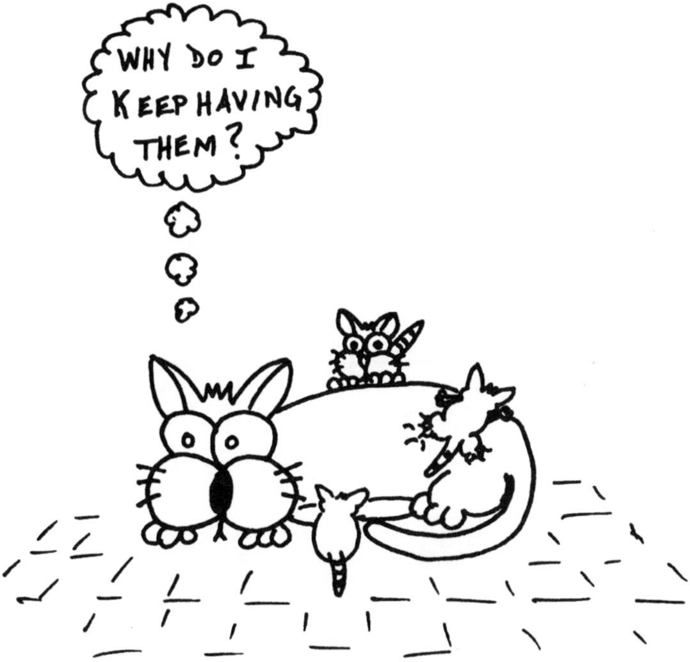
WHY DO I
KEEP HAVING
THEM?

Attack of the Kittens

Kittens will usually brave pant legs as they learn to climb. Walking around the house with a litter of kittens stuck to you can be quite tricky!

Hunting Skills

Mom Cat is their prey when they learn to hunt and attack.

137

The Big Bad "Bug" Hunter

Since mice are relatively large and quick as compared to a kitten, the kitten must practice on a smaller, less suspecting victim ...

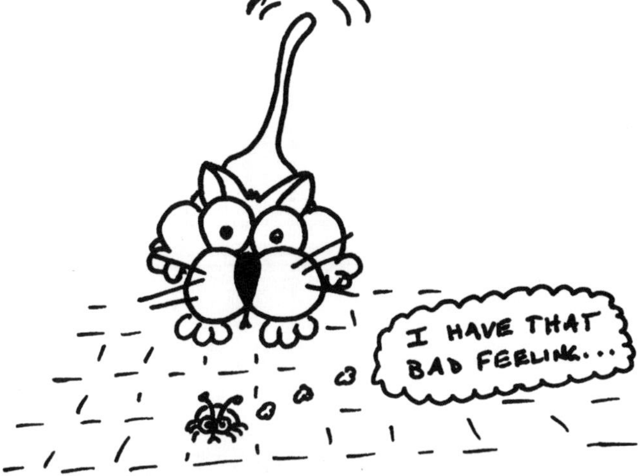
I HAVE THAT BAD FEELING...

CHAPTER 7

Kitty Fears

One Day Left . . .

Until trash pick-up. Get 'em before the garbage man does!

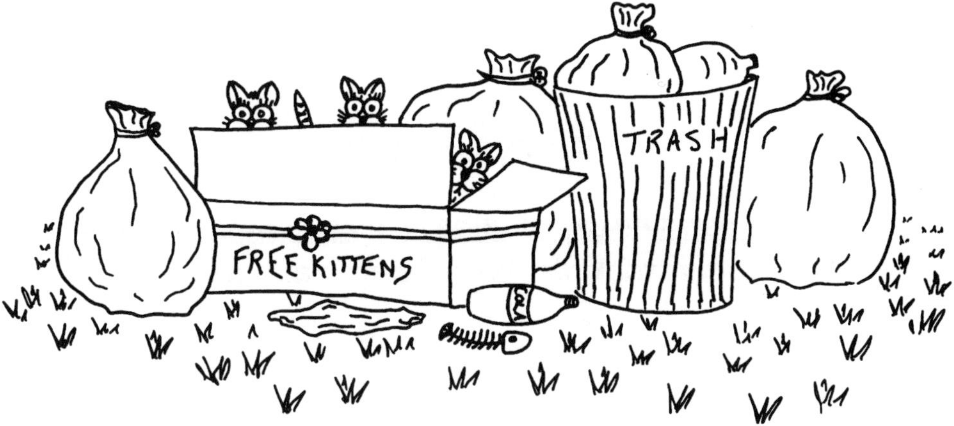
FREE KITTENS
TRASH
COLA

Kitty Crunch!

This is how the expression "nervous as a cat in a room full of rocking chairs" came about.

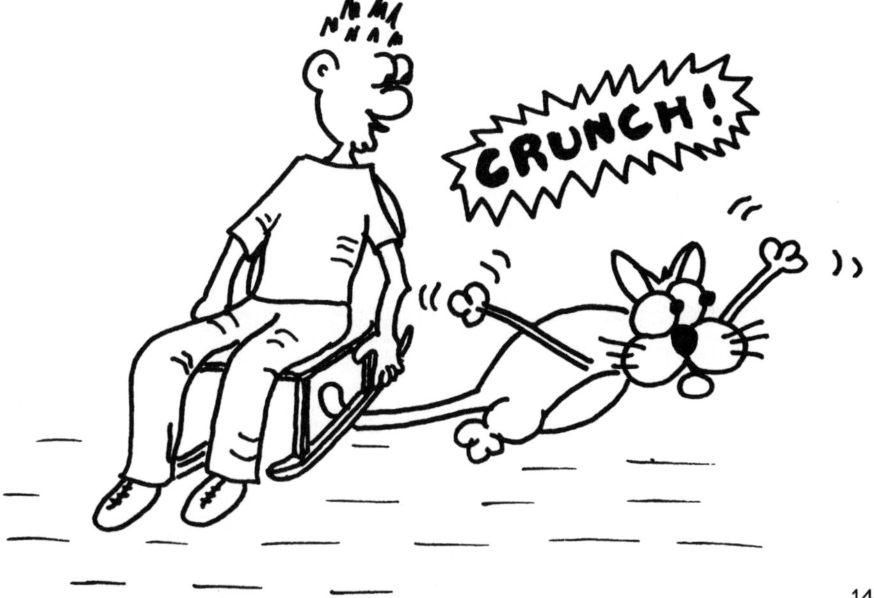
CRUNCH!

Stuck

For being such good climbers, cats seem to get stuck in trees often.

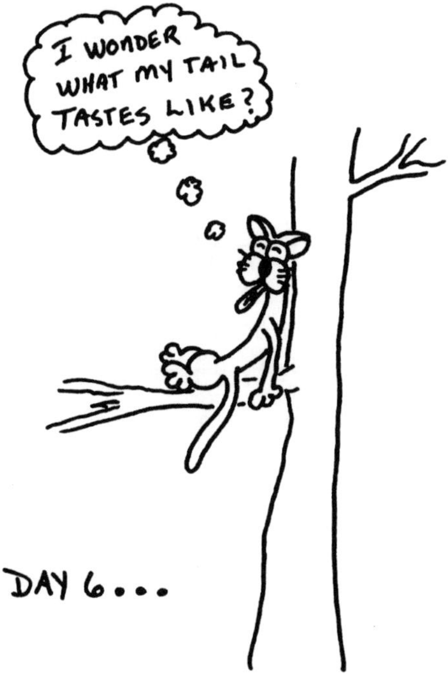
I WONDER WHAT MY TAIL TASTES LIKE?
DAY 6...

The Vet

Cats hate the veterinarian's office with a passion! You will see the happiest of cats turn white with fear at the suggestion of a visit.

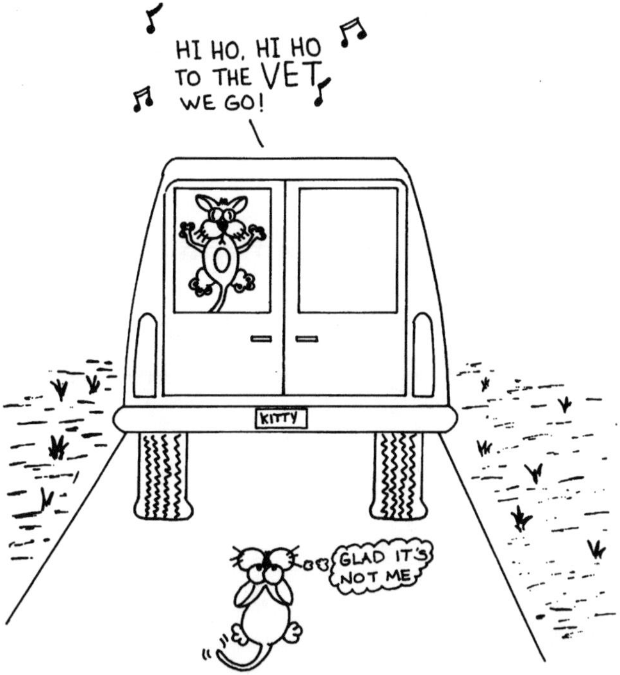
HI HO, HI HO
TO THE VET
WE GO!
KITTY
GLAD IT'S
NOT ME

Cat Carrier Battle

A cat being placed in a cat carrier usually precedes a visit to the veterinarian. That's why they fight so hard to stay out.

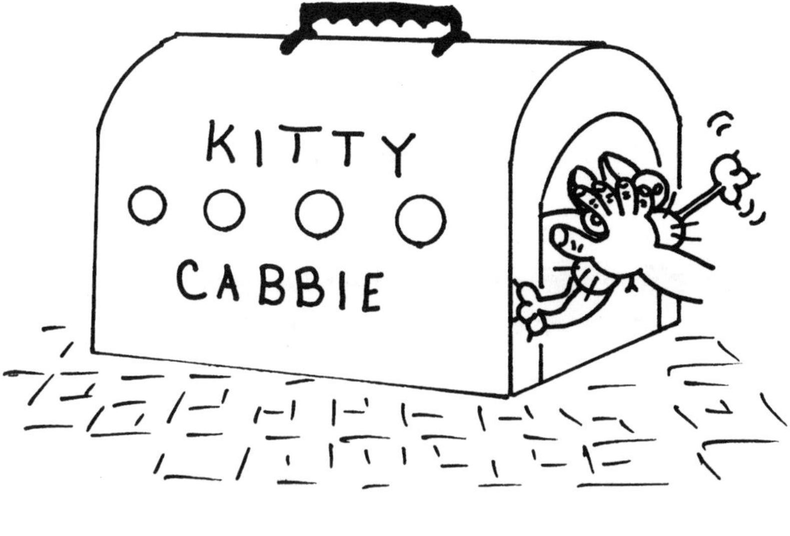
KITTY
CABBIE

Surprise!

Sometimes cats will stick their paws into holes in an effort to get at their quarry. This blind attack can sometimes backfire.

Home Too Late

Some cats don't return until the wee hours of the morning, sometimes after it begins raining out.

155

V-8 Nightmares

Sometimes cats like to sleep underneath the hoods of cars to keep warm. Too bad for kitty if the driver's in a hurry.

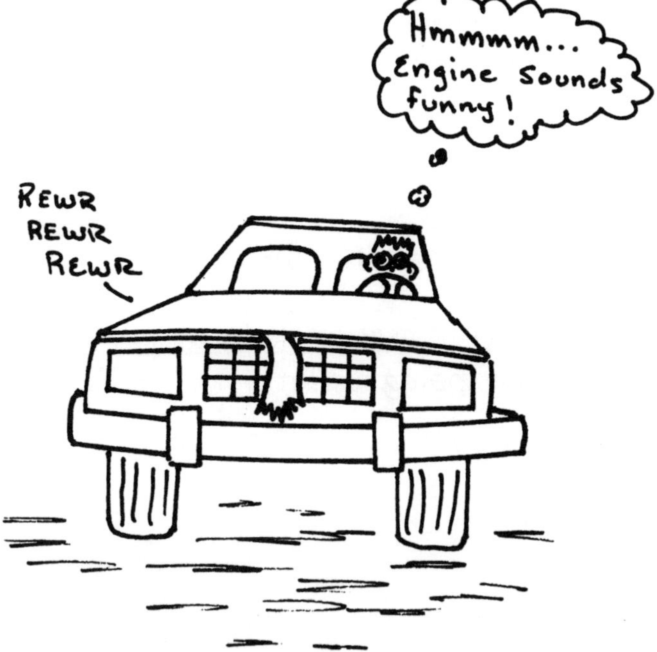
Hmmmm...
Engine sounds funny!
REWR
REWR
REWR

Defenseless

A cat losing its claws is like a skunk losing its scent or a dog losing its bite.

POOR KITTY...
THIS WILL HURT YOU
MORE THAN IT WILL
HURT ME!
HEE HEE...